Now Circa Then

by Carly Mensch

A SAMUEL FRENCH ACTING EDITION

SAMUEL FRENCH

FOUNDED 1830

NEW YORK HOLLYWOOD LONDON TORONTO

SAMUELFRENCH.COM

ISBN 978-0-573-69926-9   Printed in U.S.A.   #29898

MUSIC USE NOTE

IMPORTANT BILLING AND CREDIT
REQUIREMENTS

NOW CIRCA THEN was originally produced by Ars Nova (Jason Eagan, Artistic Director) in New York City. It was directed by Jason Eagan, with set design was by Lauren Helpern, costume design was by Jenny Mannis; the lighting design was by Traci Klainer; the sound design was by Ryan Rumery; and the production stage manager was Damon W. Arrington. The original cast was as follows:

MARGIE. . . . . Maureen Sebastian
GIDEON . . . . Stephen Plunkett

CHARACTERS

MARGIE, 26 – a shy and slightly awkward girl; more goose than swan, but with an unconventional beauty. Non-white.*

GIDEON, 27 – a hardcore history buff; passionate and youthful, with a hint of arrogance. White.

*Margie's character is scripted as Filipino-American, based on the actress who originated the role, but she can be of any race or ethnicity, really, so long as she's an unlikely casting choice for a 19th century Jewish immigrant. There are two scenes where her race is explicitly mentioned – scene 9 and scene 22. Adjust accordingly.

SETTING

A restored 19th century tenement on New York's Lower East Side, present.

The play is divided into three rooms: the **parlor** (beginnings), the **kitchen** (middles), and the **bedroom** (endings).

AUTHOR'S NOTES

This play is schizophrenically split between two worlds: the world of Gideon and Margie (naturalistic) and the world of Julian and Josephine (stylized, theatrical). Actors and designers should go to town distinguishing between these two modes. Make rules and break them as the play gets messier and the two worlds collide.

In terms of how to stylize the reenactments, the main question is how much to include the audience. Two possible broad approaches are: 1) treating these scenes like living dioramas (fourth wall; all questions to the audience are rhetorical) or 2) treating them like snippets of an actual live museum tour. In the Ars Nova production, we opted for the second. Finding moments to ad lib and engage the audience (baiting them to respond at times) without ever putting any specific audience member on the spot. If you go the participatory route, you might want to give the audience clues that they're part of the story (turning the house lights on, for example). Also, be prepared for audience members to chime in at weird times. We had one woman shout in response to Margie's question "Does anyone have any questions?" with "YEAH, WHAT'S GOING ON!?" (Good question.)

Either way, be bold. Aim high. Overshoot. Mess up. Try again.

- Carly Mensch

PROLOGUE

1.

*(Pin-spot on two people in nineteenth century costume
– MARGIE and GIDEON. They smile at the audience.
GIDEON is pert and enthusiastic; MARGIE looks vaguely
uncomfortable.)*

GIDEON. If everyone could scooch a little closer. No strangers here. Only opportunities!

(They smile and wait.)

Hello. Guten Tag. How is everybody doing today? Yeah, okay. My name is Julian Glockner and over here is my wife, Josephine.

MARGIE. Hi. I'm Josephine.

GIDEON. We are so *psyched* to see you!

Do we have any immigrants with us today? Anyone? Maybe just someone from out of town?

(If people respond – go with it and skip the next line.)

No? That's okay, we don't like to single people out.

We're all fellow travelers. Josephine and I happen to be recent travelers ourselves. That's right. We traveled all the way from a little place called "West Prussia" circa 1890, just to be here with you today, here on the Lower East Side of New York.

MARGIE. *(wooden)* Yes. Between 1815 and 1915, more than thirty million immigrants came to America. They came from places like Germany, Russia, Austria-Hungary, Italy and Romania. Oh. And Poland.

GIDEON. Our journey begins now. In this hallway.

(MARGIE *and* GIDEON *motion to the door behind them.*)

(slow, deliberate) Behind this door lies the tenement apartment Josephine and I will share for over thirty years together. Now. Let us turn the doorknob ourselves and enter into the rooms of the past...

(GIDEON *does some big, sweeping gesture.*)

(MARGIE *smiles, sort of.*)

(blackout)

PART ONE

2.

(The Parlor.)

(A room with a small fireplace, a dress form and a sewing table.)

(But also: an Exit sign, light switches and fire sprinklers.)

(MARGIE *passes* **GIDEON** *items from a large suitcase.)*

MARGIE. One pair ladies stockings.

One pair of shoes, leather.

Two candlesticks.

Three pairs of cotton underwear, men's.

GIDEON. I hope these are mine, eh Josephine?

MARGIE. One jar of pickled herring.

One photograph of our native village of Moloschnya.

(GIDEON *takes out a laminated version of the same photograph and displays it to the audience.)*

GIDEON. *(nostalgic)* Yes. *Moloschnya.*

It seems like only yesterday when we met at Jakkob the Elder's to sign our *arranged* marriage agreement, eh Josephine?

MARGIE. That's right, Julian.

GIDEON. *(re: the unpacking)* Is that it?

(MARGIE *looks inside the suitcase – it's empty.)*

MARGIE. Yup.

GIDEON. *(out to the audience)* What luck! You've caught us at a fortuitous time, travelers! Josephine and I have only just arrived in the New World.

MARGIE. America.

GIDEON. We left behind many friends and family. My mother, Irina, a dancer. My father Rudolph. The cabbage farmer.

MARGIE. We rode here on a very big boat.

GIDEON. In steerage.

MARGIE. When we arrived at New York harbor, a man loaded our mattress onto his wagon. He said he was going to give us a free ride into the city.

GIDEON. Unfortunately. That ride didn't include us.

MARGIE. Then we came here. To the Lower East Side.

GIDEON. To this apartment.

MARGIE. This room is called the "front room."

GIDEON. One day, when Josephine and I have children, they will sleep in this room.

MARGIE. Not that we have any children.

GIDEON. But we will. Some day.

MARGIE. In the future.

GIDEON. Well, near future.

MARGIE. Or distant.

(pause)

GIDEON. This might be a good time to mention that Josephine and I are *newlyweds!*
The boat-ride over was essentially our honeymoon.

*(He smiles lovingly at **MARGIE**.)*

MARGIE. *(forcing a smile back)* Yup.
I threw up six times.
And then I got lice.

GIDEON. We both got lice.

3.

(Lunch break.)

*(***GIDEON*** *reads a biography of James Madison.* **MARGIE** *eats a Pop Tart.)*

(After a while:)

MARGIE. Hi. Excuse me?

*(***GIDEON*** *looks up.)*

This is really embarrassing. I keep forgetting your name.

GIDEON. It's Gideon.

MARGIE. Hi Gideon, I'm –

GIDEON. Margie. I know.

MARGIE. Oh.

*(***GIDEON*** *goes back to reading his book.)*

MARGIE. So have you done this kind of thing before?

GIDEON. What kind of thing?

MARGIE. With the costume. And the tour groups.

GIDEON. You mean *reenactment?*

MARGIE. Sure.

GIDEON. Historical interpretation. Living history.

MARGIE. Either one.

GIDEON. Yeah, I've done a lot of reenactment.

MARGIE. You're really good at it.

GIDEON. It's kind of my thing.

MARGIE. So what other places have you done?

GIDEON. Uh, I've done Gettysburg.

MARGIE. Cool –

GIDEON. I've done Plymouth.

MARGIE. Okay –

GIDEON. I've done Salem. I've done Shaker Village. I've done Daniel Webster. I did a few Renaissance Fairs back in college. I've done two Air & Space museums. I've done five birthplaces, all politicians, all Republican. I've done the Boston Fire of 1872 and I just got back from doing this amazing hundred acre Living History Farm in Urbandale, Iowa.

MARGIE. Wow.

GIDEON. It's an addiction. My brain is like a twenty-four hour History Channel.

What's past is prologue, right? That's Shakespeare.

MARGIE. Right.

GIDEON. We all think we're like these orphans, but we're not really.

MARGIE. We…?

GIDEON. People our age. Like we're these invincible orphan children, running around big cities without any family or history of our own. But we're not, right? Orphans. We all come from somewhere. That's why I like this museum. Immigrants, man? That's like our prologue.

What about you. What's your story?

MARGIE. Well. I just moved here. To New York. I'm still a little…aggh!

Uh. I'm 26.

GIDEON. You a history major?

MARGIE. English.

GIDEON. And do you have a background in creative role play?

MARGIE. No.

GIDEON. Do you have any experience as a tour guide?

MARGIE. Nope.

GIDEON. No tour guide experience.

MARGIE. No.

GIDEON. None.

MARGIE. Nope.

GIDEON. So like…how did you get this job?

MARGIE. That woman. With the lipstick?

GIDEON. *(under his breath)* Way to go, Roberta.

MARGIE. Excuse me?

GIDEON. Nothing. She's just totally loosening her standards. Up on the third floor – you know, the 1920's apartment – she hired this Guatemalan guy who can barely even speak English.

MARGIE. Mario?

GIDEON. I think she's on some post-racial…liberal-guilt kick. No offense.

MARGIE. None…taken.

GIDEON. It's like – no one cares about *authenticity* anymore. I mean – you seem like a perfectly nice person and whatever, but Josephine – she was a 19th century Jewish immigrant. She was…

MARGIE. White?

(beat)

GIDEON. We're a *history* museum. That's our whole raison-d' etre: Making *history* come to life.

(a short silence)

MARGIE. I don't know. I think history is sort of bullshit.

GIDEON. Excuse me?

MARGIE. Like – slavery? People need to get over it already. It's not like I'm personally responsible for what a bunch of racist white guys did a hundred years ago. People should just move on already. Stop worshiping boring old facts.

GIDEON. Okay – I, um. Sorry.
I don't understand. Why would you take a job at a *museum* if you don't believe in history?

MARGIE. I told you. I just moved here. I needed a job.

GIDEON. You don't think that's…irresponsible?

MARGIE. Are you kidding? I'm eating my lunch out of a vending machine. I still don't have a place to live. So to answer your question. No. I don't think it's irresponsible. In fact – it's probably the most responsible thing I've ever done. Ever.

(pause)

GIDEON. This job. It's like super, super important to me.

MARGIE. I see that.

GIDEON. The last Josephine. She only lasted about a month. Just, FYI.

4.

(Later.)

*(**GIDEON** sits at a foot-treadle sewing machine.)*

*(**MARGIE** enters carrying heavy buckets of water. She is now extremely pregnant. She takes a seat next to* **GIDEON***.)*

GIDEON. Josephine –

MARGIE. Yes, Julian.

GIDEON. Do you know the price of potatoes this month?

MARGIE. ...No.

GIDEON. Just take a guess.

MARGIE. Uh. A dollar?

(pause)

GIDEON. *(out to the audience)* Anyone else? Any guesses? Sack of potatoes. 1890. *(field some guesses)* It's ten cents.

MARGIE. Is that a lot?

GIDEON. Are you kidding? It's insanity! Prices go up and wages go down. Don't worry though – I'm a very resourceful man.

MARGIE. Oh, well that's good.

GIDEON. It's time to be frugal, Josephine. No more of those frilly dresses you like to buy from the pages of Sears & Roebuck. We need to start watching our spending. Especially now with the baby on the way. Everything costs money, in these post-industrial times. Any idea how much I spent on this sewing machine over here?

MARGIE. Uh...hold on.

*(**MARGIE** picks up a laminated sheet of paper from the table. She quickly skims the document.)*

(reading) Twenty-six dollars?

GIDEON. Yup. And that's only cause I got it second hand from a Lithuanian street peddler.

MARGIE. *(still reading)* "This model is significantly smaller than Singer's original version. The aforementioned price includes a built-in table. For further reading, please see Singer and the Sewing Machine: A Capitalist Romance."

(looking up)

Oh.

GIDEON. The point is, Josephine. It's about *seizing* opportunities. It's about seeing your dreams ahead of you and catching them with your own custom-made...dream-catching net.

*(**MARGIE** lets out a laugh.)*

(forging ahead) In our native village, I was a lowly shoe cobbler. Here in America – I am an entrepreneur. A man of boundless potential. A man of...

*(**MARGIE** sneezes loudly.)*

*(**GIDEON** looks at her, horrified.)*

5.

(After work.)

*(**GIDEON** sits at the sewing machine, mending a pair of pants. Coincidentally, he's not wearing any himself.)*

*(**MARGIE** enters carrying a large three-ring binder.)*

MARGIE. Don't say anything. I know I fucked up.

GIDEON. Didn't say anything.

MARGIE. I've read this stupid manual like five hundred times. You're not wearing any pants.

GIDEON. Got caught on a nail.

MARGIE. I'll just go somewhere else.

GIDEON. Hey. It's your living room too, right?

*(**MARGIE** takes a seat, reluctantly.)*

MARGIE. I didn't know you could sew. In real life.

GIDEON. Eagle Scouts.
I'm also just a really resourceful person. In general.

*(**MARGIE** opens up the binder.)*

*(**GIDEON** sews.)*

(Every once in a while he looks over at her, reading. After a while:)

Can I give you some advice?

MARGIE. Let me guess: Don't suck.

GIDEON. What you're looking for – it's not in the manual.

MARGIE. What are you talking about?

GIDEON. You can read that thing cover to cover. Memorize every single footnote. Still not gonna help.

MARGIE. Thanks. That's very constructive.

GIDEON. Just saying.

MARGIE. So. What would help?

GIDEON. You really want to know?

MARGIE. Yes.

GIDEON. Stand up.

MARGIE. What?

GIDEON. Stand up.

(She does.)

So. Have you ever done any kind of acting before?

MARGIE. Acting? No.

GIDEON. This museum – we get a lot of former actors. It's like where theater people come to die.

MARGIE. I'm not an actor.

GIDEON. That's okay, that's fine.

MARGIE. Sorry – I thought the point is to be educational.

GIDEON. Yeah…Not really. I mean, people can just pick up a textbook if all they want to do is obtain information, right? There's a certain artistry I like to think. Have you ever seen *Apocalypse Now* with Marlon Brando?

MARGIE. Sure.

GIDEON. You know that scene with all the severed heads?

MARGIE. I think so.

GIDEON. I love that scene! Brando wasn't in that one, but you should really watch him. Very *instinctual* –

MARGIE. I don't understand – what is it you want me to do?

GIDEON. It's not about *doing* anything. It's about how you hold yourself.

MARGIE. And how do I hold myself?

GIDEON. Just kind of, regular. Like yourself.

MARGIE. So?

GIDEON. So. Josephine should hold herself like Josephine. Not like Margie.

MARGIE. I hate improv if that's what this is going to be. *I am a plum tree. I am a tea pot.*

GIDEON. It's not improv.

Okay. I'm going to go exit the room and then come back. Just watch.

*(**GIDEON** exits the room and comes back.)*

Notice anything?

MARGIE. Not really.

GIDEON. Good.

Now I'm going to do it again.

(**GIDEON** *exits the room once more. This time, when he re-enters, he walks with heightened energy and pep. The energized body. Yup. That's right. We all know this.*)

See the difference?

MARGIE. You're more taut, I guess.

GIDEON. Right. The first time I entered as myself. The second time as Julian Glockner – dressmaker, husband, *persona*. It's like the difference between resting on your heels and leaning forward on your toes.

MARGIE. It matters how I'm *leaning*?

GIDEON. Yes! When you don't really *inhabit* your part. When you're not really *giving* me anything, then I can't do my job. It's like a push-pull.

Your turn now.

MARGIE. You want me to exit the room and come back?

GIDEON. Yeah.

(**MARGIE** *walks listlessly out of the room.*)

(*She re-enters approximately the same.*)

Okay…So maybe focus on how you're standing.

(**MARGIE** *tries to stand up really tall.*)

Great. That's…better.

Now, relax your shoulders a bit.

(*She does.*)

Your neck, too.

(*She does.*)

Yeah, that makes a huge difference.

MARGIE. Really?

GIDEON. Uh huh.

MARGIE. I just feel more self-conscious now.

GIDEON. That'll go away.

Now maybe try layering something in. Like – is she tired? From a long, hard day of work?

(**MARGIE** *hunches her shoulders.*)

And maybe her hands are clenched, from all that sewing.

(**MARGIE** *clenches her fists.*)

And maybe she has a sense of striving. Like, a woman who is just trying to get by. Survive.

(**MARGIE** *tries to think of something to do, but has no idea. She drops the pose altogether.*)

What? What happened?

MARGIE. I feel like an idiot.

GIDEON. We're all idiots.

MARGIE. It's a comfort thing. I need to get more comfortable with the material.

GIDEON. Forget about the lines.

MARGIE. Besides. I don't even know who this woman is!

GIDEON. She's...Josephine Glockner.

MARGIE. Yeah, but who *is* she?

GIDEON. She's a nineteenth century immigrant.

MARGIE. *(starting to freak out)* But why did she move here? What is she trying to prove?

GIDEON. I don't think she was trying to prove anything...

MARGIE. It's not like this city has magical transformative powers. It's not like you move here and *poof,* you're suddenly a whole different person.

GIDEON. Sure...

MARGIE. Besides – Julian isn't perfect either.

GIDEON. I never said he was.

MARGIE. Personally, I find him a little over the top sometimes. His whole persona.

GIDEON. Character –

MARGIE. That *voice* he does.

GIDEON. Hey!

    *(**MARGIE** starts taking off her costume.)*

MARGIE. I'm sorry. I can't do this.

GIDEON. Do what?

    *(**MARGIE** heads to the door.)*

    What are you doing?

MARGIE. Just, tell Roberta I'm sorry.

    *(**MARGIE** rushes out.)*

GIDEON. *(calling after her)* Margie? Hey, Margie!

6.

*(***MARGIE*** *alone in the parlor.)*

MARGIE. Hello, I'm Josephine.

   Hi. I'm Josephine.

   Guten Tag, my name is Josephine.

   Hi. I'm Josephine.

   Hello, I'm...

   I'm...

   What's my name? Oh my god how can I forget the name part?

   Josephine! My name is Josephine. Duh.

   My name is Josephine. Hello. Please to meet you. Josephine. My name is Josephine.

   I am a strong, self-actualized independent woman.

   I am also a poor, marginalized Eastern European immigrant.

   I am...

   Damnit.

7.

(Next day.)

*(**GIDEON** is about to start. **MARGIE** rushes in and joins him, out of breath. They share a quick glance before launching into the reenactment.)*

GIDEON. This is a little segment we like to call: *Who Knew?* Who knew, Josephine, that in 1890, many people didn't use toothbrushes?

MARGIE. Who knew?

GIDEON. Good thing those women at the Settlement House came up with a song to help us remember to use them. Remember?
(singing) "Here we are coming to clean our teeth, clean our teeth, clean our teeth,
Here we are coming to clean our teeth; and we do it night and morning."
How about another round.

*(**MARGIE** joins in, reluctantly.)*

GIDEON/MARGIE. "Here we are coming to clean our teeth, clean our teeth, clean our teeth,
Here we are coming to clean our teeth; and we do it night and morning."

MARGIE. *Who knew*, Julian. That Immigrants were often called by their derogatory name; "Greenhorns."

GIDEON. Who knew?

MARGIE. Greenhorn referring, obviously, to being green. Clueless. Easily taken advantage of.

GIDEON. Who knew!

MARGIE. Who knew.

8.

(After work.)

*(**GIDEON** sweeps the floor.)*

*(**MARGIE** paces the room on a cell phone.)*

MARGIE. *(into the phone; deeply annoyed at whoever she's talking to)* I don't care. Why?…Because it's stupid…It is. It's a baby, not a Nobel Peace Prize…
Fine. I'll send her an email. I will. I will. Tell Dad I say hi. Okay. Bye. Bye.

*(**MARGIE** hangs up.)*

Am I supposed to be doing anything right now?

GIDEON. You're supposed to be cleaning up.

MARGIE. Oh. Duh.

*(**MARGIE** retrieves a bucket and some gloves.)*

(She picks up a candlestick and polishes it very gently.)

GIDEON. I thought you were quitting.

MARGIE. I changed my mind.

GIDEON. That was a pretty strong reaction, yesterday.

MARGIE. Yeah. I do that sometimes. Freak out.

GIDEON. Do you suffer from panic attacks?

MARGIE. No. I'm fine.
I guess. Sometimes I get overwhelmed.

GIDEON. That…

MARGIE. That, I don't know. That I'm living this tiny insignificant life? That I'm never going to achieve my full potential as a human being on this earth?

(pause)

GIDEON. Oh.

MARGIE. Back in Michigan. I was working for my uncle and dating this guy and living in my parents basement and I was like: really Margie? Is this really who you want to be?

*(**MARGIE** catches **GIDEON** staring at her.)*

MARGIE. What?

GIDEON. You look like someone. Remind me of them.

MARGIE. Who?

GIDEON. My mom.

MARGIE. Okay…

(**MARGIE** *picks up an old clock.*)

GIDEON. DON'T TOUCH THAT!

(*She puts the clock down.*)

That clock. It's from 1802. It was made by this really, really famous colonial clockmaker. It's super delicate.

(**MARGIE** *slowly puts down the clock.*)

MARGIE. Sorry.

GIDEON. It's okay. You didn't know.

(**MARGIE** *picks up a ceramic tureen with extra caution.*)

MARGIE. You're *really* intense about history.

GIDEON. It's…important to me.

MARGIE. I see that.

GIDEON. Modern times are boring. Besides, the way I see it, our generation is doomed.

MARGIE. Why?

GIDEON. Because we're all culturally bankrupt?

We have no tangible things to pass down to our children. No artifacts. No family heirlooms.

All we have is fleeting virtual moments.

MARGIE. Isn't that what people said with the telegraph? That we'd all turn into robots.

GIDEON. No. This is different. This is *epically* tragic.

Think about it: We keep all of our memories out in Data Storage Centers in the Midwest. In these massive cement buildings where Microsoft and Google and Facebook back up our identities. These are the temples we're constructing. Data Centers.

It's so sad.

That's why I don't have a cell phone.

MARGIE. How do you stay in touch with people?

GIDEON. I check email on my dad's computer about once a month. That's enough, trust me.

MARGIE. So your dad lives in New York?

GIDEON. Yeah. I'm sort of staying with him for a bit. Plus – Upper West – way nicer than whatever I could afford in Brooklyn.

(**MARGIE**'s *cell phone rings again. She picks it up and turns away from* **GIDEON**. *After a beat:*)

MARGIE. NOOOOOOOOOOOOOOO!!!

(*She hangs up the phone.*)

(**GIDEON** *stares at her for a moment.*)

MARGIE. What?

GIDEON. Nothing.

9.

(Two weeks later.)

*(**MARGIE** brushes her teeth, a sleeping bag on the floor beside her. After a bit, **GIDEON** enters.)*

(He watches her for a moment in horrified silence.)

GIDEON. Hi.

MARGIE. *(turning around)* Hi! Gideon. You're...early.

GIDEON. Did you...sleep here last night?

MARGIE. No.

GIDEON. I can see your sleeping bag.

(beat)

MARGIE. Okay. Here's my reasoning. I don't have enough money for both food *and* shelter. And since food is more critical to survival than shelter, it makes more sense to spend my money on that. Also, there's no commute. It's 100% efficient. Think of Lighthouse keepers. They sleep in the same place they work, and they're some of the most dedicated and passionate members of the workforce.

GIDEON. In France.

MARGIE. And...Maine.

GIDEON. How long has this been going on?

MARGIE. A few days. A week. Two weeks. Two weeks. I swear, that's it.

GIDEON. I'm going to be fired. Shit. We're both going to be fired.

MARGIE. It's not that bad! And not the bed. I didn't touch the bed.

GIDEON. I have to report this, right?

MARGIE. What? No you don't.

GIDEON. I have a reputation to uphold. I can't be... complicit...I can't –

MARGIE. Gideon.

GIDEON. You realize this violates like every rule of the museum.

MARGIE. No.

GIDEON. Uh, yeah. Pretty much.

MARGIE. Look at you – you break rules all the time!

GIDEON. Name one rule I've broken since you've been here.

(She thinks about it.)

MARGIE. Socks!

GIDEON. What?

MARGIE. Sometimes when I look down I notice you not wearing any socks.

GIDEON. Yeah, they make my ankles sweat.

MARGIE. In the Educator Manual, under the Health Code & Hygiene section, it says all Interpreters are required to wear both socks and underwear beneath their costumes at all times.

GIDEON. No one's going to care whether or not I wear socks, trust me. And I can just put talcum powder in my shoes. Problem solved.

MARGIE. Also – you go completely off-script!

GIDEON. It's a tour. It's supposed to be improvised.

MARGIE. But half the things you say aren't even in the outline.

GIDEON. That's because I have a very specific style of enactment that I have been developing for over five years now. And yeah, maybe it's a little more lax than, whatever, a Ken Burns PBS special, but that's why it's such an effective and ultimately engaging method.

Also, I've been nominated for the Society of Creative Anachronism's Founding Father Award three years in a row now, so I must be up to something.

MARGIE. Then you shouldn't be so nervous about me telling Roberta.

(pause)

GIDEON. Wow.

MARGIE. What?

GIDEON. You're a little scary when you're like this.

MARGIE. Like how?

GIDEON. Like, cornered.

MARGIE. *(softening)* Think about it. It's in the spirit of the museum. Helping people. Providing shelter to newcomers.

GIDEON. I know that… I'm not insensitive. You're just putting me in a really uncomfortable position.

MARGIE. I know that.

GIDEON. So. You're homeless?

MARGIE. No!
I've also had a shitty week. I got on the subway going in the wrong direction and I ended up at JFK airport. Which, sucked.

GIDEON. I thought you had a place in Queens?

MARGIE. I did.

GIDEON. What happened?

MARGIE. Nothing.

GIDEON. What?

MARGIE. It just didn't work out, okay?

GIDEON. Did something happen?

MARGIE. No. No.

GIDEON. *(sensing something)* What?

MARGIE. It's stupid.
Okay – so I don't really know how to say this. But. The landlady. She's this really old, senile Polish lady. She used to be a nun but now she just sits in a lawn chair outside our building. Anyhow. I think she thinks I'm Mexican.

GIDEON. What are you talking about?

MARGIE. She brings up Arizona in like every conversation. And Mexican drug cartels. And then this one time – she casually mentioned that her nephew happens to be a Minuteman.

I guess I've been confused with other Asian people. Vietnamese, usually. I'm Filipino. But never Mexican.

GIDEON. Wait. Are you saying you were…what, discriminated against? This woman kicked you out of your apartment.

MARGIE. No. She just raised the rent. Which, people do all the time in this economy.

GIDEON. How much did she raise it?

MARGIE. Two hundred percent.

GIDEON. That *fucking* woman.

MARGIE. No – she's really old. I'm probably projecting.

GIDEON. Fucking racist asshole.

You realize you can sue. You can file a formal complaint.

MARGIE. No – I don't even know if that's what happened.

GIDEON. This is New York City. This is supposed to be the most tolerant, diverse city on the planet.

MARGIE. It is.

GIDEON. My dad. He can help find you a really good discrimination lawyer.

MARGIE. No. Please. I don't want to make a big deal.

GIDEON. This is *exactly* why this museum exists. To combat things like this. To *educate* the unenlightened assholes of the world.

MARGIE. I don't want to be some *victim*. That is not who I want to be. Please. Just let it go.

(**GIDEON** *paces as he thinks about his options.*)

GIDEON. Okay. This is what I'm going to do.

I am going to slowly walk away and go hang out in the dressing room. Read a little James Madison, maybe eat a granola bar. And when I return, we'll just pretend that this never happened.

MARGIE. Really?

GIDEON. If Roberta finds out, though. I'm not going to lie.

MARGIE. Understood.

Gideon – you have no idea how much this means.

GIDEON. I'm slowly walking away.

I'm…walking away.

10.

(Enactment.)

*(**MARGIE** holds up a large textbook.)*

*(**GIDEON** stands beside her.)*

MARGIE. "In 1492, Columbus sailed the ocean blue."
"In 1492, Columbus sailed the ocean blue."
"In 14 –

GIDEON. Josephine –

MARGIE. Yes, Julian?

GIDEON. What exactly are you doing?

MARGIE. I'm learning English!

GIDEON. But why?

MARGIE. Because – we're Americans now.

GIDEON. That's right. Immigrants had to give up many aspects of themselves to become Americans, including their native language.

MARGIE. An important question to ask, however, is why?

*(turning to **GIDEON**; earnest)*

Why do we want to be Americans so badly?

Why are we willing to give up so much of ourselves?

GIDEON. *(completely taken off guard)* Well, Josephine…uh. It's the land of opportunity!

MARGIE. On paper.

GIDEON. Upward mobility?

MARGIE. For…two percent of the population.

GIDEON. Still – the *possibility* of it.

MARGIE. I think we left Prussia because we were sick of our old lives. Of who we had become.

We so badly wanted to reinvent ourselves.

*(**MARGIE** turns to **GIDEON**, dead serious, fierce.)*

Julian. I want you to know – I'm ready to *do* this.

GIDEON. Okay…

MARGIE. Really *be* Josephine.

GIDEON. Because you are, her.

MARGIE. Yes! That's what I'm saying. I'm not just some soot-faced pathetic outsider. I'm – a person.

GIDEON. Of course.

MARGIE. Yeah. So. I'm *ready.* I just wanted to say that.

(realizing she's gotten carried away; out)

Sorry.

(GIDEON *looks at her. Impressed. Intrigued.)*

GIDEON. No.

(silence)

Uh. Let's meet over by the fireplace, folks.

11.

(After work.)

*(**MARGIE** and **GIDEON** change out of their costumes.)*

GIDEON. I like what you did back there.

MARGIE. Really? I thought you were going to scream at me.

GIDEON. No. It was raw. Honest.

MARGIE. Did you know she was my age?

GIDEON. Well, people had shorter life spans back then.

MARGIE. She also came from a really small town. Like me.

GIDEON. Sure.

MARGIE. Maybe I'll check out some books. Go to the library. Can you –

(She gestures to a hard-to-reach clasp on her costume. He helps her with it.)

GIDEON. Yeah. Hey. What are you up to tomorrow night?

MARGIE. Hanging out at the sketchy youth hostel I'm staying at.

GIDEON. First Friday of every month a bunch of us gather in the museum after hours.

MARGIE. Oh.

GIDEON. Grab some beers. That sort of thing.

MARGIE. Actually. I would love to meet the other people who work here. I still don't really know anyone.

GIDEON. I figure. Since you're part of the team now.

MARGIE. Yeah. Okay. What time?

GIDEON. People usually start arriving at around 8 o'clock. Eight thirty.

MARGIE. Cool. I'll be there!

*(**GIDEON** has finished changing.)*

GIDEON. You coming?

MARGIE. I'm just going to finish up here.

GIDEON. Alright.

> *(He starts to leave, then stops himself.)*

> And, really good job today.

MARGIE. Thanks.

> *(**GIDEON** exits.)*

> *(**MARGIE** stands alone for a moment.)*

> Hello. I'm Josephine.
> Nice to meet you. I'm Josephine.

> *(She relaxes.)*

> *(finally, in her own voice:)*

> Hi. I'm Josephine.

> *(This works.)*

12.

(Late night.)

*(**MARGIE** and **GIDEON** sip fruity wine coolers.)*

(The kerosene sconce has been turned on low.)

MARGIE. Do you think anyone else is coming?

GIDEON. I swear this wasn't intentional.

(They both sip their drinks.)

MARGIE. *(re the beverage)* What is this?

GIDEON. Tahitian Sunset.

MARGIE. Mmm.

GIDEON. I got it from the Yemenese deli on the corner. Yemen-aye? Yemeni?

MARGIE. This neighborhood is so weird.

GIDEON. Weird because…

MARGIE. There are like a bajillion different nationalities, and yet we, an immigrant museum, never really talk about any of that.

GIDEON. Sure we do.

MARGIE. How?

GIDEON. It's implied. You know. Julian. And Josephine. Their story.

MARGIE. Okay. But what does that really mean?

GIDEON. You…ask a lot of questions.

MARGIE. Sorry.

GIDEON. No. It's good. I like – questions.

MARGIE. *(laughing)* Okay…

GIDEON. Besides – it's important. Knowing where you're from.

MARGIE. Why?

GIDEON. Because. Your heritage –

MARGIE. Is eating corn on the cob and watching Harrison Ford movies?

GIDEON. Really?

MARGIE. Yes.

GIDEON. Oh.

Well. Fuck heritage then.

(He holds up his drink.)

To corn on the cob and Harrison Ford!

MARGIE. Here here!

GIDEON. To…Tahitian Sunset!

MARGIE. Tahitian Sunset!

GIDEON. To…moving to New York! To starting over and… eating Pop-Tarts for lunch.

(They clink; drink.)

You're doing a really good job here, by the way.

MARGIE. Really?

GIDEON. When you first got here I thought you were massively under-qualified. But you definitely bring something…unique. So. I apologize if I judged you.

MARGIE. It's cool. I judged you, too.

GIDEON. You did?

MARGIE. Yeah.

Are you kidding?

Yeah.

(They drink.)

GIDEON. Why did you say you left Michigan?

MARGIE. Because I didn't want to be a pharmacist's assistant my whole life?

Also. My sister got pregnant.

GIDEON. Congrats.

MARGIE. No. That's what everyone says. Like it's some sort of feat. Personally, I find it depressing. She's 28 and now her whole life is over. Done. She doesn't even want to go back to work. Just stay home and have babies. It's gross.

(She takes a huge gulp.)

Ugh! I can't end up like that. Promise me – I will never end up like that.

GIDEON. Okay.

MARGIE. Seriously.

GIDEON. I…promise. You will not stay at home and have babies.

*(**MARGIE** downs the rest of her drink. She paces.)*

MARGIE. Whatever. Look at me: I work at a *museum.*

GIDEON. Hey – me too.

MARGIE. I'm a *tour guide.*

GIDEON. Educator.

MARGIE. *(with anxious energy)* I want to…do things. You know?

GIDEON. Sure.

MARGIE. Big, important things.

GIDEON. You should. You should totally do that.

MARGIE. I want to be passionate about something. Give myself completely. You know?
Like – fully commit, with my whole being. Like…like…

(a realization)

you.

GIDEON. Me?

MARGIE. Yes. You are so…How did you become so passionate about history?

GIDEON. Uh. My mom, probably. She taught history at Columbia.

MARGIE. See?! Even your family does stuff.

GIDEON. She wrote this controversial book in the 80s that made her super famous. It's on every major grad school reading list. She's dead. Sorry, I don't know if I mentioned that.

MARGIE. Oh. I'm so –

GIDEON. Nah, it's cool. She died a long time ago. When I was in high school.

MARGIE. Must have been hard.

GIDEON. My dad. He still really hasn't gotten over her. He just sits and watches women's basketball every night.

MARGIE. Do you want to talk about it?

GIDEON. You would have really liked her I think. You actually remind me a little of her.

MARGIE. Yeah, you said that.

GIDEON. That kind of pioneer woman. With messy hair. Strong, but, also really human. Like one of those people you meet and you're like *now that's a person. That's somebody who's really lived.*

*(Suddenly, **MARGIE** leans in and kisses him.)*

(a long, long silence)

Wow. So was that like, a pity kiss?

MARGIE. No.

GIDEON. So then –

MARGIE. I don't know. It just came over me.

GIDEON. Okay.

(They sit with this.)

Do you think, it might come over you again? Just, in terms of gauging expectation.

MARGIE. I don't want this to change anything.

GIDEON. Sure, of course. We have to work together.

MARGIE. I'm not looking for a relationship. The last guy I dated – I kind of lost myself in him.

GIDEON. Sure.

MARGIE. And I'm not going to sleep with you.

(They start making out, desperately. Knocking things over.)

(after a while:)

What if? No. Nevermind, it's stupid.

GIDEON. What?

MARGIE. I was just thinking.

Would it be totally weird –

What if we changed into our costumes?

GIDEON. Like. Our work clothes?

MARGIE. Is that an awful idea?

GIDEON. I'm sorry. What?

MARGIE. Just – for fun.

GIDEON. Okay. Yeah.
Wait. Shit. *Fuck.* I took it home with me. It's at the dry cleaners.

MARGIE. Oh. Nevermind.

GIDEON. Sorry.

(pause)

GIDEON. But...*you* could. If you want. If that's something you're interested in. No pressure though.

MARGIE. Yeah?

GIDEON. Only if that's something you want. I am in no way explicitly requesting this.

MARGIE. Just – something different.

GIDEON. Sure.

MARGIE. I'll be right back.

GIDEON. Alright. I will wait here. Sit.

*(**MARGIE** exits to the dressing room.)*

*(**GIDEON** sits nervously and fidgets. He unbuttons his collar. Buttons it back up. Unbuttons it again. Buttons it back up. He takes a huge chug from his cooler. Maybe he contemplates putting on some music.)*

*(**MARGIE** re-enters, wearing her costume.)*

MARGIE. I didn't put on the apron.

GIDEON. You look –

MARGIE. Like Josephine?

*(She approaches **GIDEON**.)*

GIDEON. I'm uh...I'm gonna go turn off the light.

*(**GIDEON** turns off the lamp.)*

(blackout)

End of Part 1

PART TWO

13.

(Five months later.)

(The kitchen.)

(A cramped room with a cast-iron stove, pots and pans.)

(A small table.)

(Laundry lines criss-crossing the space.)

(MARGIE, in a slip and stockings, stands over the stove, stirring a pot.)

(GIDEON, in undershirt and suspenders, sits at the kitchen table reading the newspaper.)

(A domestic scene.)

(After a long silence, the two turn to face the audience.)

MARGIE.   GIDEON.
  Immigrants –   Sweatshops –

MARGIE. Sorry!

GIDEON. No! You first.

MARGIE. No. You go.

GIDEON. Please. I insist.

MARGIE. I was just going to say:

  Immigrants spent a lot of time in the kitchen.

GIDEON. Yeah they did!

(They smile out at the audience.)

Hey. Come here.

MARGIE. *(blushing)* I'm – working.

GIDEON. Come on.

    *(***MARGIE*** nods to the audience.)*

    (re: the audience)

    Trust me. They've seen married people before.

    (She takes a seat on his lap.)

    Tell them what we did yesterday.

MARGIE. No!

GIDEON. All Sunday. We just stayed in bed.

MARGIE. Not *all* day.

GIDEON. We were like – breakfast? No, thanks. Lunch? Yup, we'll take that right here.

MARGIE. We went out for lunch.

GIDEON. We had these amazing – what would you call them?

MARGIE. Pasticotti.

GIDEON. These Italian pastries. With all this cream.

MARGIE. They were very good.

GIDEON. Italian people. What's up with them?

MARGIE. What do you mean?

GIDEON. They're so good at cooking. No wonder they're so fat, right?

MARGIE. *(hitting him)* Julian!

GIDEON. I'm kidding. I love Italian people.

    Mobsters?

    I'm kidding!

    (They smile and sigh out to the audience.)

    *(***MARGIE*** stands.)*

MARGIE. I should get back.

    (She heads back to the stove.)

GIDEON. I always think kitchens are very warm places. Not just because of this *authentic* coal-burning stove we have here. Something about food and family…

MARGIE. But also, routine.

GIDEON. Routine?

MARGIE. All this cooking. And cleaning. It's so easy to forget, outside this room, you're still a person. You're still this living, pulsating, breathing thing.

(GIDEON stares at her admiringly.)

GIDEON. Josephine.

MARGIE. Yes, Julian.

GIDEON. I love you!

MARGIE. I love you, too.

(MARGIE turns back to the stove.)

(GIDEON continues gazing at her, adoring her, forgetting himself.)

(He catches himself.)

GIDEON. *(out)* I'm sorry. Uh, what were we saying?

14.

(After work. Cleaning up. They're already mid-conver-sation.)

GIDEON. ...Because history should be *immediate*. It should feel like getting slapped in the face.

MARGIE. You don't think we're getting too...personal?

GIDEON. No way.

MARGIE. All that. *I love you, I love you.*

GIDEON. We love each other, so.

MARGIE. But Julian and Josephine.

GIDEON. They loved each other, too.

MARGIE. I just can't imagine them being like that.

GIDEON. Why not? They were human beings...

MARGIE. Sure.

GIDEON. You want us to portray them as what, miserable, downtrodden people? Is that it?

MARGIE. No, definitely not.

GIDEON. Poor them. Poor Julian and Josephine.

MARGIE. They're not *victims*, clearly. Maybe just less...affectionate?

GIDEON. Margie. They had five kids together. I don't think *affection* was a problem.

MARGIE. But they're middle age now.

GIDEON. So?

MARGIE. So. People grow old. They grow bored with each other.

GIDEON. Are you getting bored with me?

MARGIE. No.

GIDEON. Besides. Boredom's a middle class thing. Julian and Josephine? They fucking, clung to each other. Clasping each other's naked bodies in the cold paucity of their lives. Why do you think immigrants had so many kids?

MARGIE. That is *not* why...

GIDEON. I know. I'm kidding. Hey. Dinner tonight. Order in?

MARGIE. Let's go out.

GIDEON. Really?

MARGIE. We haven't gone out in months.

GIDEON. We could play a board game.

MARGIE. We always play board games.

GIDEON. How about I cook you something?

MARGIE. You're going to cook.

GIDEON. Yes. I will cook you an elaborate non-spaghetti meal. I'll even break out the placemats.

MARGIE. Fine. But no Prussian music.

GIDEON. No Prussian music. I hate Prussian music.

(beat)

Hey – come here.

MARGIE. No. You come here.

(He does. He puts his arms around her waist.)

GIDEON. Look at you. You're all sweaty.

MARGIE. Thanks.

GIDEON. No, I like it. And whatever, I'm sweaty too. It's hot in here.

(She reaches over and picks something off his shoulder.)

MARGIE. You have something –

GIDEON. What?

MARGIE. Oh. It's just dandruff.

GIDEON. Is it bad? To be this comfortable with someone?

MARGIE. No. I don't know.

GIDEON. Were you this comfortable with your last boy-friend?

(beat)

MARGIE. Whatever. What about you?

GIDEON. What do you mean?

MARGIE. Other girlfriends.

GIDEON. I haven't had any other girlfriends.
Come on. You knew that.

MARGIE. Yeah. I guess. I just assumed.

GIDEON. I'm not ashamed.

MARGIE. You shouldn't be. I've only really dated two other people. And neither of those were – like, adult.

GIDEON. Think Josephine dated people? Before Julian.

MARGIE. I thought they had an arranged marriage.

GIDEON. Yeah. Probably better that way anyway.

MARGIE. Are you kidding?

GIDEON. Yeah. They didn't have to go through the whole charade of meeting people. Flirting. Putting on fake identities. They could just – commit. Start building a future together.

(beat)

(suddenly) Oh right! I almost forgot.

MARGIE. What?

GIDEON. I've been carrying this around all day.

(GIDEON *pulls a crumpled tissue out of his pocket.)*

MARGIE. Why…?

GIDEON. It's just something that made me think of you. Here:

MARGIE. What is it?

(He hands her the tissue. She unwraps it.)

GIDEON. *(not waiting for her to figure it out)* It's a brooch.

MARGIE. *(overwhelmed)* It's…
Did you buy this?

GIDEON. No. It was my mom's.
I think it may have been her mother's or something. It's a family heirloom. My dad said I can give it to you. May I?

(He pins it to her.)

MARGIE. It's like, I've been pinned.

GIDEON. I figured. Since there are no girls in my family.

(She opens her mouth to protest, but then changes her mind.)

MARGIE. I…Thank you. It's beautiful.

15.

(Next day.)

(MARGIE, *now wearing the brooch, irons.)*

(GIDEON *reads the newspaper as before.)*

GIDEON. Josephine.

MARGIE. Yes, Julian?

GIDEON. Listen to this Headline:

(reading)

"Man Bludgeoned to Death By Errant Meat Cleaver."

MARGIE. Huh.

GIDEON. "Wife is key suspect."

MARGIE. Wow.

GIDEON. It says here, the motive for murder was "noisy jaw-bone."

"His jaw made this awful clicking sound when he slept. So I killed him."

MARGIE. It's always the little things, isn't it?

GIDEON. What a crazy time we live in, eh Josephine? The nineteenth century.

MARGIE. Pretty crazy.

GIDEON. You would never think of doing that to me, would you?

MARGIE. Kill you? No.

GIDEON. Well that's a relief.

(out)

Right, folks?

(He reads. She irons.)

The American Dream...

MARGIE. Yup.

GIDEON. A good job. A good family.

MARGIE. Well, it's not *ideal.*

GIDEON. It's pretty close.

MARGIE. Or, you know, a compromise.

GIDEON. God Bless America.

MARGIE. Yes. God Bless America.

(a beat)

Ow! DAMNIT –

GIDEON. What? What's going on?

MARGIE. Nothing. I burned myself.

GIDEON. On the stove?

MARGIE. No, on the pantry. Yes, the stove.

GIDEON. Do you need ice?

MARGIE. That iron. It's so…fucking heavy.

GIDEON. It's eight pounds. Like most irons of the time…

MARGIE. How are people expected to work in this stupid heat.

GIDEON. I can get you some water.

MARGIE. No, it's fine.

GIDEON. I'll just go down to the pump.

MARGIE. I'm fine! Okay? Just stop.

GIDEON. Okay…

Are you mad at me?

MARGIE. No. I'm.

(recovering, out to the audience)

It's my own fault.

16.

(The kitchen table.)

*(***MARGIE*** reads New York Magazine.)*

*(***GIDEON*** eats an apple, loudly.)*

(An air of slight boredom.)

(This goes on for an uncomfortably long time.)

GIDEON. I think I might grow a beard. What do you think?

MARGIE. Go for it.

GIDEON. Something, 1850s.

MARGIE. *(reading)* Listen to this: every Thursday night they have free jazz concerts at the Met.
There's champagne and you get to walk around the exhibits. Jerry Seinfeld supposedly goes.

GIDEON. We hate jazz.

MARGIE. So.

GIDEON. I don't understand. Why would you go to something if you don't like the activity?

MARGIE. Because I've never been to the Met.

GIDEON. It's not that exciting.

MARGIE. That's because you grew up here. You take things for granted.

GIDEON. Well, that's what real New Yorkers do. We take things for granted.

MARGIE. Are you saying I'm not a real New Yorker?

GIDEON. You're not.

*(***MARGIE*** is slightly offended.)*

But that's a good thing, trust me. New Yorkers are assholes.

(This doesn't help.)

*(***MARGIE*** goes back to her magazine.)*

Hey. I was thinking. We should get our own place.

MARGIE. What?

GIDEON. Instead of you staying over at my dad's house every night.

MARGIE. Why? Did he say something?

GIDEON. No. I just think we're adults. We shouldn't have to sneak around every night. Maybe some place with a backyard. Grow our own vegetables.

MARGIE. I don't have the money right now.

GIDEON. I can cover the first few months.

MARGIE. I don't want your money.

GIDEON. That's not what I meant.

MARGIE. Gideon – I can't move in with you.

GIDEON. Why not? We already technically live together. We spend like every waking hour together.

MARGIE. I am well aware of that.

GIDEON. Plus. We're already married.

MARGIE. Gideon!

GIDEON. Kidding. Totally kidding.

MARGIE. I don't even know your middle name!

GIDEON. It's Alexander.

MARGIE. See? I didn't know that.

GIDEON. That's good. We still have more to learn about each other.

MARGIE. I can't move in with you.

GIDEON. Why not?

MARGIE. We haven't lived yet. Done anything.

GIDEON. I've done stuff.

MARGIE. Me. I haven't done anything. Accomplished, anything.

GIDEON. So, do it. Accomplish something.

MARGIE. I'm trying.

GIDEON. You should apply for that assistant curator position.

MARGIE. What?

GIDEON. There's a sign in the staff room. I got you an application.

MARGIE. What? I'm not even qualified.

GIDEON. You're super qualified.

MARGIE. I don't even know if this is what I want to do – work in a *museum* for the rest of my life.

GIDEON. So? It's a good opportunity.

MARGIE. Well, I don't want it.

GIDEON. You don't even want to think about it?

MARGIE. No.

GIDEON. Wow. That's open-minded.

MARGIE. This isn't my dream. Working at museum. This is your, whatever.

GIDEON. Then why are you still working here?

MARGIE. Because. I don't know.

(softening)

I'm sorry – I like working here. I shouldn't have said that. I'm just being crazy.

GIDEON. I might apply. If you don't.

MARGIE. You should.

GIDEON. There's more freedom. Plus you get to decide the exhibits.

MARGIE. Yeah, you should definitely apply.

(GIDEON *takes a final bite of his apple.)*

GIDEON. Hey – how much time do we have?

MARGIE. A few minutes.

GIDEON. I got to take a shit.

(GIDEON *tosses her the half-eaten apple and exits.)*

(MARGIE *sits, staring at the apple, disgusted.)*

17.

(A few days later.)

*(***MARGIE*** *sits over a bucket, scrubbing clothes on a washboard. Or with a wooden agitator, if you can find one.)*

(She scrubs. The more she scrubs, the angrier she gets.)

*(***GIDEON*** *enters with a handful of bills and receipts and an account book; he sits down at the table and begins going through them.)*

GIDEON. Josephine?

MARGIE. Yes.

GIDEON. Nothing.

I was just saying hi.

MARGIE. Hi.

(They work.)

GIDEON. Josephine?

MARGIE. WHAT!? Why do you always have to say my name. Josephine. Josephine. Josephine. I'm right here.

GIDEON. I feel like we don't really talk any more.

MARGIE. We talk all the time. We're talking right now.

GIDEON. Why are you so angry?

MARGIE. I'm not. I'm busy. I'm working.

GIDEON. Is this because of your sister?

MARGIE. What?

GIDEON. Your sister who just gave birth in our hometown of Moloschnya.

MARGIE. What does my *sister* have to do with any of this?

GIDEON. Maybe you feel bad you weren't there?

MARGIE. I sent her a postcard.

GIDEON. Sometimes. I wonder if you're projecting your hatred of your sister onto a hatred of domestic life in general,

MARGIE. I do not *hate* my sister.

GIDEON. Of course.

MARGIE. *(getting angry)* And I don't hate "domestic life in general."

I just find it pathetic that people succumb to social norms just because, whatever, something's been done that way for hundreds of years. That like "home" has so much *meaning* to people and that domestic bliss is somehow this *inevitable* goal. Like it's destiny.

GIDEON. History *is* destiny.

MARGIE. Oh, please.

GIDEON. What?

MARGIE. You say all these *things*. These *empty* things.

GIDEON. No...

MARGIE. Yes.

I wish you could hear yourself. How ridiculous you sound sometimes. How cliché.

(They work.)

GIDEON. Josephine.

MARGIE. *(tired)* Yes, Julian.

GIDEON. I was just wondering.

MARGIE. What?

GIDEON. Last night.

(Beat. MARGIE sits up a bit.)

Where were you, exactly?

MARGIE. Where was I when?

GIDEON. I woke up in the middle of the night and you weren't there.

MARGIE. I was there.

GIDEON. No, you weren't.

MARGIE. Really?

GIDEON. Nope.

MARGIE. Oh. Right. I had to go out for something.

GIDEON. For what?

MARGIE. *(looking out at the audience)* We shouldn't...you know. Not here.

GIDEON. I think we should. *Here.*

MARGIE. It's just.

I had some errands to run, that's all.

GIDEON. At eleven o'clock at night?

MARGIE. There was a fabric situation. I forgot to tell you about it. It's a long story.

GIDEON. Give me the short version.

MARGIE. Well, we ran out of fabric for the week. So I went to see Johan, our fabric guy. And he was like, *oh, we're also out of fabric.* And I was like, *really?* And he was like, *we're getting another shipment in if you can come back later tonight.*

GIDEON. Huh.

MARGIE. Yeah. I can't believe I didn't tell you about it.

GIDEON. About the fabric situation.

MARGIE. Right.

(beat)

GIDEON. It's just interesting, though, because. I found this ticket stub in your pocket.

(He takes a ticket stub out of his pocket.)

(MARGIE looks up, caught.)

(GIDEON holds up the stub.)

Also – we get our fabric delivered from a supplier. Not Johan. We haven't used him in years. I think he might even be dead.

(He reads the stub.)

"Grizzly Bear Meets Beer Street."

(He looks up to see her reaction; she has none.)

With headliner: "Sergeant Dutchface and the Newsboy Quintet."

(silence)
(He shows the ticket stub to the audience.)

What do you think that could be?

(MARGIE shrugs.)
(GIDEON studies the ticket.)
(They stare at each other, face-off style.)

18.

(Meanwhile, back in the real-world:)

GIDEON. Sgt. Dutchface?

*(**MARGIE** shrugs, defiantly.)*

Really, Margie?

Really?

(More silence, more stare downs.)

19.

(Back in reenactment land:)

GIDEON. So you're saying…Vaudeville!

MARGIE. Uh huh.

GIDEON. As in: Clog dancing. Blackface. Stand-up comedy.

MARGIE. Yes. I go to Vaudeville.

GIDEON. That's the best you could come up with?

MARGIE. I didn't "come up" with anything. It happens to be the dominant form of populist entertainment in the 19th century.

GIDEON. I know that, Josephine.

MARGIE. It's a vital part of the Lower East Side's history.

(under her breath)

I can't believe you went through my things.

GIDEON. *(whispering back)* It was on the dresser.

MARGIE. *(whispering)* It's mine.

GIDEON. *(whispering)* It's my apartment.

MARGIE. *(whispering)* It's my life.

(Back to their normal, museum voices.)

GIDEON. So you were saying. *Vaudeville.*

MARGIE. Yes.

GIDEON. The whole 2nd Avenue circuit!

MARGIE. That's right.

GIDEON. Why didn't you just ask me to come?

MARGIE. Because you hate that kind of thing!

GIDEON. How do you know?

MARGIE. You hate anything that's loud and modern. You would have called it "gaudy" or "grotesque."

GIDEON. Maybe.

MARGIE. And I happen to like going out. I like the people.

GIDEON. Meaning, you prefer the company of strangers to the company of your own husband?

MARGIE. No. I prefer being part of the World instead of retreating from it.

GIDEON. The World being…crazy drunk people.

MARGIE. The World being…millions of strangers, people other than you and me.

That's the point of living in a city. Just F.Y.I.

GIDEON. Yeah, I understand how cities work.

MARGIE. I want to live my life. Get drunk sometimes and stay out late and make bad decisions. Not furrow away in some house with a boyfriend and a vegetable patch.

GIDEON. I don't need to grow vegetables!! That was just an example!!!

*(Suddenly, **MARGIE** swipes everything off the kitchen table. Plastic food and silverware go flying.)*

What are you doing!?

MARGIE. I hate this table! I hate this fruit. And this stupid bowl. …

GIDEON. That's authentic…!

MARGIE. *(holding a doily)* And this…what is this? I don't even know what this is. It's ugly. I hate it.

(She throws it on the ground.)

(more frantic now) This whole kitchen – I hate it. It's suffocating me. Ugh!

(She grabs the laundry lines and rips them down, creating a tangled mess.)

(She stands – out of breath, a little wild-eyed.)

GIDEON. *(slowly)* Who…are…you?

MARGIE. I am Josephine *fucking* Glockner.

(Scary.)

20.

(MARGIE paces the room sipping a Starbucks iced beverage. Something super obnoxious. Think whipped cream. Think Venti.)

MARGIE. *(speaking a hundred miles a minute)* …She's stuck. She's trapped in this routine and this life and this marriage. She came here with all these hopes and aspirations. She's disappointed in herself. I get these things. I understand her disappointment.

GIDEON. *(distracted)* Uh huh.

MARGIE. She needs to break out. Make changes in her life.

GIDEON. *(still staring at the coffee)* I'm sorry. I can't tell if you're trying to obliterate my soul or if you're just accidentally sipping the most evil beverage on earth.

MARGIE. What?

GIDEON. You know I feel about Starbucks.

(GIDEON eyes her – Is she doing this on purpose?)

MARGIE. What do you think about my theory on Josephine?

GIDEON. Yeah. Sure. Go with it.

MARGIE. No, really though. I want your opinion.

GIDEON. I think…it sounds like a perfectly competent and viable approach to the character.

MARGIE. Yeah, right? I think so. It was such a *release.* Playing her this way.

GIDEON. Sure.

MARGIE. This has nothing to do with you, you realize. With Julian. Julian's great.

GIDEON. Oh, well that's good.

MARGIE. I was thinking. For the bath-tub moment. Maybe Josephine contemplates *drowning* her own infant son. What do you think about that? With her bare hands. Like…*grrr.*

GIDEON. Can we stop talking about this?

MARGIE. Oh. Sure.

GIDEON. It's kind of all we ever talk about. Here. On break. At the apartment.

MARGIE. You're right. Boundaries.

(pause)

(Then, unable to help himself:)

GIDEON. And I really don't think Josephine would do that by the way. Infanticide? She's not fucking, Lady Macbeth. She's a regular, moral person.

MARGIE. You think I'm playing her wrong?

GIDEON. No. I didn't say that.

MARGIE. Be honest.

GIDEON. Honestly. I think she's maybe getting a little self-indulgent. Maybe.

MARGIE. Self-indulgent?

GIDEON. "I hate laundry!" "I feel trapped."
Yeah, a little.

MARGIE. She's angry.

GIDEON. Okay. But why?

MARGIE. Because she's stuck.

GIDEON. So is Julian.

MARGIE. It's different.

GIDEON. Why is it different?

MARGIE. Because.

GIDEON. Because, you, Margie, are terrified of ending up like that?

MARGIE. No!

GIDEON. Because what then? Because you're mad at me? Because you're mad at yourself?

MARGIE. No. This has nothing to do with me.

GIDEON. You're right!
This museum has absolutely nothing to do with you.

MARGIE. What is that supposed to mean?

GIDEON. It means. This museum is not about you or Josephine or whether or not you're playing her like some insane character in a classic melodrama.

MARGIE. So what is it about?

GIDEON. It's about *two* people. About how they go through life together.

About how they figure out how to be *decent* to each other even as times get rough.

How maybe they lose their way sometimes, but how they help each other make it through and ultimately *enrich* each other's lives.

And then how ALL of that somehow fits into the larger HISTORY of a place called The Lower East Side CIRCA EIGHTEEN NINETY!!

That's what I think.

(beat)

Also. I didn't want to bring this up – but it's weird, when you're having sex with someone, to call them by the name of a character they're playing at a museum.

MARGIE. I do not do that!

GIDEON. Yes. You do it all the time. You did it last night.

MARGIE. No…

GIDEON. Feels great.

MARGIE. You're the one who told me I need to *inhabit* my part.

GIDEON. Yeah, not completely supplant your own identity.

MARGIE. I'm…figuring a lot of stuff out.

GIDEON. It's not that hard. It's called: Be Yourself. Stop trying on a million different personas.

MARGIE. I'm not –

GIDEON. Yes. You are so insecure –

MARGIE. *(knee-jerk)* You fart in your sleep!

GIDEON. What?

MARGIE. You do. I never say anything. But you do. And it's gross. It's like a train whistle.

GIDEON. That's real mature.

MARGIE. And you have psoriasis. Your elbows flake off all over the bed, like these little pieces of skin, which is really not very romantic.

GIDEON. I don't understand. If I'm so repulsive, why did you make out with me in the first place?

MARGIE. We were drunk. Whatever. I would have made out with anyone that night. I would have made out with a tree.

GIDEON. You would make out with a tree?

MARGIE. Oh, shut up.

GIDEON. So that night – You were just using me? Was that it?

You were homeless, sleeping on the floor and figured, I bet that kid Gideon will take me in. He looks innocent enough. He seems vulnerable.

MARGIE. No!

GIDEON. What then? Are you saying it was a mistake? These past few months?

MARGIE. No.

I don't know what I'm saying. You're just, springing this on me.

GIDEON. It's called having a *conversation*, Margie. It's called dialogue.

MARGIE. All I know is I came to this city to be on my own. To be independent for once in my life and become a version of myself I'm actually proud of. But instead I ended up exactly where I was before – in some *relationship*, spending half my time lying around your apartment like a rag doll and the other half sneaking around, doing all the things I know you secretly disapprove of.

GIDEON. I don't *disapprove* of you going out at night!

MARGIE. Yes, you do – you're very judgmental.

GIDEON. You should just tell me. Gideon – I want to go out.

MARGIE. I tell you all the time! You don't listen. You're stuck in this cocoon of like history and…I hate this, I hate that.

GIDEON. What. So this is my fault?

MARGIE. No. It's no one's fault.

The point is – I got distracted. I got…sidetracked somehow.

GIDEON. Sidetracked from what?

MARGIE. From…I don't know.

GIDEON. Then how can you be sidetracked from it?

(**MARGIE** *shrugs, having no answer.*)

Alright.

I'm just going to say everything I'm thinking. Lay out all my cards on the table.

Number One. I like you. In fact, I love you. I think I've made that pretty clear. So, whatever I'm about to say should somehow be predicated on that fact.

Number Two. That first night we had together. That was one of the greatest nights of my life. Period.

Number Three. I have psoriasis. You're right. I do. I have this cream I'm supposed to put on it but I never use it. It smells weird and it's cold and I just don't care about those kinds of things and honestly I'm a little surprised that you do but that's besides the point.

Four. Okay, I'm going to stop the list format now.

Bottom line. What the fuck? You used to be this amazing girl and now you're this self-absorbed, crazy monster person who drinks Starbucks all the time and talks about killing imaginary children. That first night, you talked all about how you wanted to do something important. I was like, Wow, this girl is going to change the world. This girl is going to do so many noble things.

But you haven't. You've just kind of sat around feeling sorry for yourself and wallowing in the entrapped domestic psyche of "Josephine." Which is weird, since, Josephine lived in a time before feminism and you don't have to be like that. Also – you keep complaining about how you're lost and don't know what to do with your life even though Roberta's given you this like amazing opportunity and you're just wasting it. You're throwing it away.

GIDEON. *(cont.)* Okay, I think I'm done.

Oh. Also. I should have gone with you to that thing at the Met. You wanted to go and I shouldn't have been such a jerk about it. I'm sorry.

(a long silence)

MARGIE. I don't love you.

I used to, I think. But. I don't anymore.

(silence)

GIDEON. That's it?

MARGIE. I'm sorry.

GIDEON. Wow.

Okay.

MARGIE. Also. I think you might be in love with your dead mother, which is a little weird.

(silence)

GIDEON. Huh.

MARGIE. I'll come get my things later this weekend. I think that would be best.

GIDEON. Yeah.

I'm gonna –

I think gonna go.

MARGIE. Gideon –

GIDEON. No. I think I should…

Yeah.

*(**GIDEON** exits; leaving **MARGIE** alone onstage. She stands in the mess she's made – proud, angry, hurt.)*

End of Part II

PART THREE

21.

(The Bedroom.)

(The most intimate and claustrophobic of the three spaces.)

(A bed, a dresser, a pair of stockings draped over a chair.)

(MARGIE enters to find GIDEON sitting on the bed tying his shoes. She freezes upon seeing him. They share a glance before turning out and launching into the reenactment.)

MARGIE. Hi everyone –

GIDEON. *(cutting her off)* Let's start.

(Uh oh.)

In 1908, Julian Glockner comes down with Tuberculosis.

MARGIE. What??

GIDEON. Tuberculosis. Consumption. The White Plague. For those of you who don't know, Tuberculosis is a disease of the lungs. Small tubercles form inside the mucous membranes, causing you to slowly drown in a pool of your own blood. Ralph Waldo Emerson once described it as: "a mouse *gnawing* at your chest."

MARGIE. Gideon.

GIDEON. What?

MARGIE. Are you okay?

GIDEON. I'm dying, *Josephine.*

MARGIE. Not...yet.

GIDEON. It's a long process.

MARGIE. Maybe we should tell them about the bedroom?

GIDEON. *(back to the audience)* The funny thing about Tuberculosis is that, historically, it has all this social stigma. It was a *poor* person disease. An immigrant, disease. But also, it was a reflection of a person's constitution. Like – *delicate* people. Sensitive people.

MARGIE. This bedroom –

GIDEON. They know what a bedroom is.

MARGIE. Sure…But it's architectural…

GIDEON. *(to the audience)* How about it guys? Do you know what a *bedroom* is? Do you know what kind of things go on in here?

MARGIE. This mattress is pretty interesting! Its filled with horsehair.

GIDEON. Let's talk about *death.*

MARGIE. Note the authentic hand-made quilt, a gift from Josephine's great Aunt.

GIDEON. Death gives a person perspective. It's like a window into the people around you.

MARGIE. You're not *dying.*

GIDEON. Yes I am. And you know what? This illness, being confined to this one room – it was like having a new pair of eyes.

MARGIE. But also, it's a space of intimacy.

GIDEON. What?

MARGIE. The bedroom.

GIDEON. Why don't you just stab me?

MARGIE. What?

GIDEON. *Intimacy?*

MARGIE. Yeah – I just meant. It's the room where people live the most private part of their lives.

GIDEON. I think it's time to take a break.

MARGIE. We're in the middle of –

GIDEON. How about everyone takes a step into the hallway for a few minutes? Check out the rockin' stairwell!

MARGIE. They've already seen the stairwell.

GIDEON. Have they? Right, okay. I think I'm going to step out then. Get some air.

(on his way out; to **MARGIE***)* You suck.

*(***MARGIE*** faces the tour, at a loss of how to handle this.)*

MARGIE. *(to the audience)* Hi…everyone.

This is…

Uh.

So this is the bedroom.

This is…

This is the bed.

This is where they slept.

In the bed.

(pause)

Wow. This is surprisingly hard to do alone.

Does anyone have any questions? That might be… anyone? No. Okay.

(She sits down on the bed.)

So, a woman walks into a doctor's office and she says: "Doctor, my arm hurts in two places. What should I do?" And the Doctor replies: "Don't go to those places."

That's an old Vaudeville joke.

Nobody has any questions? Nobody?

22.

(After work.)

MARGIE. Tuberculosis.

GIDEON. It's in the Manual. Look it up.

MARGIE. I know what TB is.

GIDEON. Leading cause of death in the nineteenth century. Plus – the real Julian. He died of TB. That's how he died.

MARGIE. Yeah, but the tour is supposed to end before then.

GIDEON. "Supposed" to. Since when has that mattered?

MARGIE. No one wants to see Julian get sick and die.

GIDEON. Why not?

MARGIE. Because. It's depressing.

GIDEON. Life is depressing.

MARGIE. No it's not. You're just saying that.

GIDEON. It can be.

MARGIE. That's because you, Gideon, are currently depressed.

GIDEON. I am not, depressed. I'm heartbroken. I don't know if you know this, but my heart was broken.
And who does this? Who comes to work the Monday after breaking up with someone?

MARGIE. Okay I admit, I said some really stupid things.

GIDEON. The main thing being: I don't love you?

MARGIE. Yes.

GIDEON. So does that mean, you do love me?

MARGIE. ...No.

GIDEON. You realize that's a pretty damaging statement to say to someone, just F.Y.I.

MARGIE. I do.

GIDEON. And...?

MARGIE. And...I feel really crappy about it. I feel awful.

GIDEON. But?

MARGIE. I don't know what you want me to say. This is hard
    for me too. I think you're a great guy. You're funny.
    Passionate. But. Now we're in this other place and we
    have to figure out how to work together.

    (beat)

GIDEON. I'd like the brooch back.

MARGIE. Oh. Okay.

GIDEON. It's a family heirloom, so, I probably shouldn't
    hand it out to just anyone.

    (**MARGIE** *takes off the brooch and hands it to* **GIDEON**.)

    Also. I think one of us should consider moving to a
    different floor.

MARGIE. I don't want to move. I like Josephine.

GIDEON. Well, I like Julian.

MARGIE. So then.

GIDEON. So.

    (Détente.)

    I was here first, you realize.

MARGIE. Yeah, and I have more emotional legitimacy.

GIDEON. Because…

MARGIE. I know what's it like to start over in a new place.
    Also. I'm…you know, a minority.

GIDEON. Wow. Did you just…?
    What happened to, "Corn on the cob. Harrison Ford."

    (**MARGIE** *shrugs.*)

    You don't even consider yourself Filipino.

MARGIE. Yeah, but other people do.

GIDEON. This is such bullshit.

MARGIE. Also. I took your advice and I'm applying for the
    curatorial position. So. It would look bad to ask for a
    transfer.

GIDEON. I can't believe this. You're applying?

MARGIE. It's a really good opportunity.

GIDEON. Wow.

Of course. Of course you're applying.

(beat)

MARGIE. So I guess I'll see you tomorrow then?

GIDEON. Yup. Can't wait.

MARGIE. Okay.

GIDEON. Yup.

MARGIE. Great.

23.

(Next day.)

(MARGIE addresses the tour from the bedroom.)

(GIDEON, brooding, abstaining, reads the paper alone in the kitchen.)

MARGIE. Last Saturday, there was this awful fire at the Shirtwaist Factory over on Washington Street.

(GIDEON coughs loudly from the other room.)

The managers – they locked the doors to the stairwells and many women were trapped inside. Can you believe that? The top three floors –

(GIDEON coughs up more phlegm over the next segment.)

(MARGIE forges on.)

This family who lives in the building. Their daughter, she worked there. How awful, right? There's going to be a demonstration next week. I think I might attend. WHAT are you doing?

(GIDEON stands up and drags himself over.)

GIDEON. I'm sick, so, I need to lie down.

Please, continue.

(He coughs one final time in her ear and lies down in the bed.)

MARGIE. I was telling our guests about the Triangle Shirtwaist incident.

GIDEON. Of 1911.

MARGIE. Yes.

GIDEON. Julian, me. I die in 1910. That's one year before... 19...11.

MARGIE. What?

GIDEON. Sorry. Public records.

Unless you're like...a psychic. Are you..?

MARGIE. No.

GIDEON. Oh.

Night Josephine.

(GIDEON goes to sleep, triumphant.)

24.

MARGIE. You embarrassed me out there!

GIDEON. I'm doing exactly what you were doing with Josephine.

MARGIE. You're being shitty.

GIDEON. I'm making it about me.

MARGIE. Lesson learned.

GIDEON. I'm not trying to teach you a lesson. I'm trying to give Julian what he deserves.

MARGIE. By killing him.

GIDEON. By finishing his story. He needs closure, Julian. He's in mourning.

MARGIE. For himself?

GIDEON. Yes. For his brief, truncated life. He was a tragic figure, Julian.

MARGIE. Is this about your mom?

GIDEON. You always bring up my mom!

MARGIE. No, I don't.

GIDEON. This is about Julian.

MARGIE. Also – the Triangle Shirtwaist Factory is totally part of this tour.

GIDEON. Not anymore.

MARGIE. You can't just make that decision.

GIDEON. Yes, I can.

MARGIE. Roberta, she'll find out.

GIDEON. Roberta hasn't come upstairs once in the year and a half I've worked here.

MARGIE. Last week, you said some things that were painful for me to hear. You said that I needed to stop feeling sorry for myself and suck it up and actually care about something already.

GIDEON. Yeah?

MARGIE. You were right.

> And so I am now making a conscious decision to change that. To *engage* here, to use this opportunity and like, go for it.

> But you. Right now you are desecrating the thing that you love.

> And – as your friend – I think you should think about that. About if this is how you want to behave. Because if it is. If it is. Then. Maybe this isn't really what you want to be doing with your life.

(silence)

(GIDEON *sits down on the bed, stunned.)*

MARGIE. I'm going to get lunch. Want anything?

GIDEON. *(quietly)* No.

25.

(**MARGIE**, *alone.*)

MARGIE. I'm sure he'll just be another minute.

(She waits.)

He hasn't been feeling well. You know, the TB.

(She waits.)

I've been thinking a lot about this city. About why people move here. Why I moved here.

Why do so many people gravitate to this one place? Is it just money? Jobs? That can't be it, right? There has to be...

Refugees – I guess they come here for asylum. And actors. Lot of actors...

(She looks over at the door and then at the time.)

This city – it's so big. Where I'm from – there are only like two thousand people. Everybody knows everybody. Here – it's like we're all strangers. We're all pursuing these individual...we're all *chasing* these...

Which makes it so easy to get lost, you know?

To forgot yourself.

And, to hurt people.

It's so easy to hurt people.

(beat)

I'm getting off-track.

But okay...listen to this. This is going to blow your mind.

(She pulls out a handful of photocopies.)

I got these from the Public Library. I've been spending a lot of time at the library now that –

They're from the Department of City Planning. Listen to these numbers.

Out of the 8.2 million people who live in New York; 37% of them are foreign born. That's almost three *million* people. Right? Isn't that crazy?

MARGIE. *(cont.)* And do you know what the top groups are?
It's like Jamaica, Guyana, the Dominican Republic.
Puerto Rico. Ecuador. Trinidad. Columbia. China.
India. India's on the rise.

(on a roll now)

Also. Did you know that Italians are dying off in New
York? Yeah, it's true. Italian people are leaving or dying
off in huge numbers, especially in Bensonhurst. It's
crazy. An entire population is in the middle of being
replaced. It's called population churn.

Are any of you Italian?

Yeah, people aren't just coming. They're also leaving.
Almost as many people come to New York each year
leave. So it's like a giant revolving door.

Yeah.

It's so exciting, right? I had no idea.

(Looks at the door – **GIDEON** *is obviously not coming.)*

Looks like Julian will not be joining us this afternoon.

So. If everyone could just move a little closer. There
are no strangers here, right? Only opportunities.

26.

(A few days later.)

MARGIE. You're quitting?

GIDEON. Put in my two week notice.

MARGIE. That's not what I meant –

GIDEON. I know.

MARGIE. What happened to applying for the assistant curator position?

GIDEON. I need to get out of this place. Try something different. Maybe Europe.

MARGIE. What are you going to do in Europe?

GIDEON. Climb a mountain. Maybe grow a beard.
Did you know I've never been outside the continental
U.S.?

MARGIE. Really?

GIDEON. How messed up is that for a history major? I've
been to Pearl Harbor but I've never been to France or
Germany.

MARGIE. Is this what you want?

GIDEON. Russia. Never been to Russia.

MARGIE. Gideon?

GIDEON. China.

MARGIE. Gideon – just stop for a second.

GIDEON. I don't know what I want. That's the whole point.

(After a bit:)

I went for this walk. I think I walked the entire length
of New York City.

MARGIE. Me too. I mean, I've been spending a lot of time
by myself, thinking.

GIDEON. I visited my mother's grave. Like, way out in
Staten Island.
When I was there, I saw this guy, this man, and he was
facing a tree. And I realized that he was…pissing. Yeah,
just peeing on a tree. Nonchalantly. And I screamed

at him. I was like *Dude, you can't do that! You can't fucking PISS in a GRAVEYARD! IT'S A GRAVEYARD. THERE ARE PEOPLE BURIED HERE YOU FUCKING ASSHOLE. THIS IS SACRED GROUND.*

MARGIE. Did he respond?

GIDEON. No. He just gave me this look. Like he knew some secret that I didn't know.

(beat)

MARGIE. I didn't tell anyone you haven't been showing up. I figure you I owe that much.

GIDEON. That was – very decent of you.

MARGIE. You should, though. Come back.

GIDEON. Nah – it's time for this cowboy to mosey on.

MARGIE. It's a two person job, remember? I can't do it by myself.

GIDEON. Julian's dying. Josephine doesn't need him anymore.

MARGIE. He's part of the history, right?

GIDEON. I don't know if I even believe in that anymore.

MARGIE. In what?

GIDEON. *History.*

MARGIE. What are you talking about. You love history.

GIDEON. No. Like putting on a costume…?
I don't even know what that word means. *History.*
History.
His-tory.

MARGIE. It's just a word.

GIDEON. This morning. I was walking around Seward Park. And I sat down on this bench across from the statue of who I assume is Seward. And I was staring at him. At this old, bronze bust of this dead statesman. And I was like:
Why? Why did we erect a statue for you?
Why, statues?

GIDEON. *(cont.) Really, why? Talk to me. Tell me why I am so obsessed with you.*

You stupid old statue. Tell me why you're here. Tell me. Tell me.
And then I stood up, and I went up to the statue and I just, kicked it.

MARGIE. You kicked a statue?

GIDEON. Yeah. I kicked it really hard. I think I broke my toe on the base.

(MARGIE can't help but smile.)

What?

MARGIE. You kicked a statue.

GIDEON. Yeah. He deserved it!

(She laughs.)

It's not funny.

MARGIE. Yes, it is.

GIDEON. I was angry.

Okay, maybe it's a little funny.

(He laughs a little too.)

(They laugh together a moment.)

*(Then: **GIDEON** switches. He suddenly becomes very serious.)*

I've been obsessed with this thing for so long: History. Capital H. But I have no idea why. I don't even know what it is. I just keep doing it. Like on autopilot.

MARGIE. You're right. Maybe you should try something else.

GIDEON. Maybe I could be a pencil maker.

Thoreau. His family made pencils.

Or a teacher. I could be a good teacher.

MARGIE. Yeah, go for it.

GIDEON. Did you know. Museums – the earliest ones, back in the seventeenth century. They were called "Wonder Cabinets." Cabinets of wonder.

MARGIE. And what were they?

GIDEON. Lot of bizarro curiosities. Dead fetuses. Works of art. Inventions.

Maybe that's what I'll do. Open my own Cabinet of Wonder. "Gideon's Emporium of Amazingness."

Where people can just come and wonder about things. No answers. Only questions.

And crackers! There would definitely be free crackers.

MARGIE. I would totally come to that museum.

GIDEON. Yeah?

MARGIE. Are you kidding? Crackers?

(They sit.)

GIDEON. My mom – She was kind of annoying.

MARGIE. What?

GIDEON. My dad likes to say she lived with us physically, but her brain lived in a different century. She loved her students, but, at home, she was like, shut off.

MARGIE. Really? I always thought. They way you talk about her –

GIDEON. No.

Jill.

That was her name.

27.

(**GIDEON**, *still in his street clothes, lies on his death-bed.*)

(*They are mid-scene.*)

GIDEON. I'm dying, Josephine.

(*Cough. Cough.*)

MARGIE. Can I get you anything?

GIDEON. No. I'm good to just to lie here. Let the TB toxins soak in.

MARGIE. A hot water bottle? Some food?

GIDEON. Just sit with me.

(**MARGIE** *pulls up a chair next to him and sits.*)

Maybe you can rub my forehead?

(**MARGIE** *begins to very slowly rub his forehead.*)

Josephine?

MARGIE. Yes, Julian.

GIDEON. Do you think...if we had met under different circumstances. Things might have turned out differently...

MARGIE. Maybe.

GIDEON. Really?

MARGIE. I think we were very young when we met.

GIDEON. I'm scared.

MARGIE. Of what?

GIDEON. Dying.

MARGIE. Everyone's afraid of that.

GIDEON. Are you?

MARGIE. Not really.

GIDEON. What are you scared of?

MARGIE. The opposite. Dying while you're still alive. Maybe that's the same thing though.

GIDEON. I'm scared of that too.

MARGIE. Yeah?

GIDEON. Yeah. Like – *Why did I even contemplate buying this cell phone? I hate people with cell phones. I don't want to be like that.* Yeah. I think about that stuff all the time.

(pause)

Can I kiss you?

MARGIE. I don't know if that's such a good idea.

GIDEON. Because I'm diseased?

MARGIE. Because...

(gesturing to the audience)

You know.

GIDEON. They've seen married people before. Plus, I want to remember what it's like to kiss you. Before I fade into the darkness of the unknown.

MARGIE. Just...one.

GIDEON. Of course.

(She leans in and kisses him gently.)

(beat)

(with a huge smile)

I'm ready to die.

MARGIE. What?

(He dies instantly.)

Julian?

(No response.)

(He's dead.)

*(**MARGIE** looks at his body for a moment.)*

(Then, slowly, she pulls the blanket over him. She gives him a final kiss on the forehead then stands to address the audience.)

(She takes a moment to find her words.)

(When she does, she speaks with confidence and maturity.)

MARGIE. *(cont.)* In the years after Julian's death, I will take over various aspects of the garment shop we set up in our tiny tenement apartment. I will become a very shrewd businesswoman. In fact, I will become one of the first female clothing contractors documented on the Lower East Side. I stopped going to Vaudeville every night. I did all the bookkeeping. I cut back on expenses. And eventually, I was able to support myself and my five children.

I was an incredible woman, I think.

Will be, I hope.

(blackout)

End of Play

www.ingramcontent.com/pod-product-compliance
Lightning Source LLC
Chambersburg PA
CBHW070642120726
47909CB00004B/1542